THE ONE THING YOU'D SAVE

BY LINDA SUE PARK

THE ONE THING YOU'D SAVE

ILLUSTRATED BY
ROBERT SAE-HENG

Clarion Books
An Imprint of HarperCollins*Publishers*
Boston   New York

All rights reserved. For information address
HarperCollins Children's Books, a division of HarperCollins Publishers,
195 Broadway, New York, NY 10007.

clarionbooks.com

The text was set in Adobe Garamond Pro.
Hand-lettering by Robert Sae-Heng
Book design by Celeste Knudsen

Library of Congress Cataloging-in-Publication Data is available.
ISBN 978-1-328-51513-1

Printed in the United States of America
2 2021
4500836307

To my WNDB and SCBWI families,
with love and appreciation —L.S.P.

To my sister, Myra —R.SH.

"Imagine that your home is on fire. You're allowed to save one thing. Your family and pets are safe, so don't worry about them.

Your Most Important Thing. Any size. A grand piano? Fine."

———— ✳ ————

For once we got *good* homework, not useless stuff like worksheets.
Best part is, Ms. Chang says we don't have to write anything down,
just think about it so we can discuss it with everyone.

We're supposed to pretend there's a fire, and we can save just one thing.
Ms. Chang says size and weight don't matter—it could be anything.
And don't worry about family or pets, they're already safe. Phew!

Makes things harder, though, 'cause I would've saved my nana first.
Arthritis—it hurts her to walk. If I tried to get her out,
I'd have to hurry her up and tell her she doesn't need her good hat.

Wonder what May's taking. Maybe I'll give her a call—
HEY, THAT'S IT! MY PHONE! I'll need it to tell all my friends,
and besides, somebody's gotta call 9-1-1, right?

——— ✳ ———

One thing? That's impossible. How can I ever pick just one thing?
I've got so much stuff I'd want to take. My books, for a start.
My graphic novels and my manga, my Calvin and Hobbes—

heck, my Neil deGrasse Tyson books, seven all by themselves!
I couldn't pick a favorite, every one of them is awesome.
Oh man, I hate this, I'm never gonna be able to decide.

———— ✳ ————

"Promise you won't think it's stupid?"
"How can I promise that, girl,
when you didn't tell me what it is yet? You tell me first,
then I tell you what I think, and you want me to be honest, right?"

"Okay. It's a sweater."
"A sweater? Which one—oh no. Not that one—"
"Which one? Bet you're wrong."
"It's that nasty blue cardigan, right?
You can't be serious! Why would you take that ugly thing?"

"I don't care that it's ugly—"
"But you hardly ever wear it!
I mean, when I can't find my phone, it's super annoying,
but that sweater, you wouldn't even miss it, so why save it?"

"If you lose your phone, you can always just get another one.
All your stuff gets stored in the cloud, right? But my one gran,
she's gone, my other gran's eyes so bad she can't knit anymore,

so there's never gonna be another sweater like it
in the whole history of the universe, not ever.
Things that you can't go buy another one, that's what you gotta save."

"All right, scholars, let's get started. I hope you all did some good thinking. Please remember to be respectful to your classmates during this discussion. Also remember

that this is just an exercise. If there were a *real* fire, you should just get out safely and not worry about your things. Understood, class?"

"UNDERSTOOD. YASS."

"Okay. Who's up first? Ron?"

"Ms. Chang, you didn't say when the fire happens, if it's day or night.
Because if it's day, I know exactly what I want to take,
but if it's night, I'd have to take something way different.

So for daytime, I'd definitely grab the program of the game
I went to last summer, Mets-Cubs, *signed* by the best player ever:
Pete Alonso, Pete Alonso! Sometimes I touch his signature

just to make sure it's still there. But if the fire's at night,
I'd have to grab my glasses from the bedside table,
because without them I wouldn't even make it to the door."

———— ✳ ————

"My sketchbook. It always has a pencil in the spiral.
I love drawing dragons. Huge wings, sharp claws, their tails and scales.

I could draw the fire, 'cause I've already drawn, like, a million flames."

———— ✳ ————

"C'mon, people—you hear me,
you gotta be real about this!

If a fire burns everything up,
you're gonna need money. A *lot*.

Am I the only one here with any smarts?
MY DAD'S WALLET. DUH."

———— ✳ ————

"It's not like it's cute or anything. Truth, it's kinda ugly.
Muddy blue, way too big for me, all droopy in the sleeves.
But sometimes things are so ugly they're cute, know what I mean?

Ages ago my gran knitted a sweater for my dad.
He wore it and wore it and wore it right out. Then my other gran,
who lives with us, unraveled it and knitted a new sweater

for me. So I'd save that sweater. Both grans and my dad—
maybe this will sound silly, but when I'm wearing it,
it's kinda like all three of them are keeping me warm."

———— ✳ ————

I bet I know what Natalie's taking—that animal collection.
With the kitten I gave her. Tan, with brown ears and brown paws
and a brown tail curled around its teeny-weeny feet. So cute!

Never told her this, but I had to open four boxes of tea
in the Key Food—pig, dog, dog, before I got the kitten.
I opened the plastic wrapping but I didn't touch the tea bags,

but the manager saw me and got really mad and yelled,
made me buy all four boxes. Good thing I had enough money.
Twelve bucks for that dumb cat! But then I got this great idea,

and what I gave Nat was this big box full of tea bags
and she had to dig through to find that little bitty kitten
looking up at her with blue eyes and she screamed, she was that happy.

—— * ——

This is easy. If there's a fire, I'd walk out with nothing.
Not a dang thing. Come see it your own self, place is a total dump.
Be a great day for me. Be glad to see it burn down.

—— * ——

My plaque. We worked for six months,
Shareen and Carly and me,

documenting every step
of how and where we collected

one hundred meteorites
from the soil in gutter runoff.

The plaque says District Science Fair,
2nd Place, in shiny letters.

Did Mae Jemison start like this?
Or Ellen Ochoa? We proved that

the dirt on the streets around here
holds chips and flakes from real stars.

——— ✳ ———

"But if I take books, I'll have to leave my game cards behind. Know how *long* it took me to collect them? And the Crimson Phoenix I only just traded for, I haven't even played with it yet!"

CRIMSON PHOENIX

WING SLAP

UNIVERSE

"Oh no. Don't you go there, Jay.
We stopped with those cards ages ago!"

"Yeah, Jay, give up that baby stuff—"

"That's enough. Class? We protect . . . ?"

"WE PROTECT, AFFECT, RESPECT
ONE ANOTHER!"

"Thank you. Who's next?"

"Ms. Chang, is it okay if—does *one collection* count?
I keep them together, on one shelf, all ninety-three of them.
Ninety-three china animals. They come free in boxes of tea."

"Ninety-three, that's a lot, Nat! How long've you been collecting them?"

"That's impressive, Natalie. And yes, I think a collection
can count as your one thing. Would you like to tell us more?"

"I started six years ago. I have the whole farm set,
doubles of the rooster and the horse, triples of the pig.
The dog set is so cute: Scottie and boxer and Shetland sheepdog.

Zoo set: I don't have the lion, but I have the lioness.
The endangereds, so hard to find, I only have three:
panda, Siberian tiger, ivory-billed woodpecker."

"It seems like a great way to learn about animals, too."

I hadn't thought of it like that, but Ms. Chang is right.
Who even knew there was an ivory-billed woodpecker?

My favorite is the Siamese cat Sandra gave me last year
for my birthday. I'd been trying to get it for ages!
Best friends know that kind of thing. It was the best present ever.

———— ✳ ————

The program. The one from the game me and Ronny went to,
really early so we could go right down to the field seats
and hang out there and watch the Mets take batting practice.

Then Pete Alonso finished up and started walking back
to the clubhouse, and I'm the one who saw him leaving the field
and ran to the rail and stood right there and held up my program

and just when he got near, Ronny caught up and stuck *his* program
out over the rail. And Pete signed it and then kept walking
and didn't sign mine. Not his fault, he can't sign everything,

it's Ronny's fault, he shouldn't have pushed ahead of me,
I'm still mad about it. I know he felt bad and he said,
"Man, I never thought he wouldn't sign yours, too," but you could tell

he was so way glad to have Alonso's autograph,
he wasn't *that* sorry. But here's the thing: Ronny had a pen,
not a marker, so already it's getting all faded

and kinda smudged, too, from him touching it. But when I called out,
"Please, Pete Alonso, sign mine, too!" he looked over his shoulder
and sort of waved and then smiled at me—at *me,* not Ronny,

so if there was a fire, I'd grab my not-signed program, because
it's from the day that Pete Alonso looked at me, right at my eyes,
and that's not ink or paper, it's for real, so it can't ever fade.

———— ✳ ————

"My bedroom rug. Quit laughing, Ty,
till you hear why first.

If someone comes out of the building
on fire, screaming,

I'm all ready with the rug.
And yell at them, 'STOP, DROP, AND ROLL!'

Ms. Chang said that *family's* safe.
Lots of other folks in my building,

like Mr. Richards? He's so old
and—and slow, he'd catch fire for sure!

He's burning up, I got that rug,
I save him, I'm a hero!"

"Hero? Shoot, that only happens in the movies. Not in real life."

"Okay, I know what you're saying. But what *I'm* saying is,
if there's a *chance* to be a hero, I'm gonna be ready."

———— ✳ ————

What I really want to take Ms. Chang might not like that much,
'cause it might sound dumb to her. I mean, I know they're just sneakers,
even if they are the coolest sneakers on the planet,

the kind Jeremy Lin wore when he scored thirty-eight points
against the Lakers—I've seen the highlights like a hundred times.
But it's not exactly the sneakers. It's me saving every cent

for months and months—I didn't buy a single thing, no apps,
no music, and when we went to Mickey D's no burger,
not even a Coke, and James sick of me mooching his fries

until finally I saved enough. Except I forgot about
the bleeping sales tax. But Mom, when the salesman said the total,
she saw my face and had a good laugh and then she came through for me.

So clean, and the shiny parts almost glowing, and no feet smell—
at first I almost didn't want to mess them up by wearing them.
Now they're broken in but I still wipe them down every night.

Maybe it wouldn't sound too dumb if I explained it right—
Chang's pretty cool. Besides, I got another good reason:
I put those babies on my feet, it's like, see ya later, fire.

———— ✳ ————

I went to the ocean once.
So big it made me feel small,
but in a good way, all the bad stuff
small too. I found a shell there,
a whole one, not chipped or cracked.
It's not very big, but it's perfect.

Last October, gray and cold.
No swimming, not even wading.
The waves—maybe this won't make sense,
but it's true—they're always changing
but always the same, and they're loud
without being noisy.

I keep that shell in my pocket,
trace the swirl with my finger
whenever I don't feel so great.
Makes me think of the ocean,
waves washing out the bad stuff
in my head. Some of it, anyway.

——— ✳ ———

Everyone's talking about their stuff, trying to decide
what they should take. They don't know what I know, Ms. Chang neither,
even though she said don't take anything if there's a fire for real.

They don't know that when the smoke starts curling in under the door
and you remember not to touch it, not to let all that smoke in,
and you get from the bed to the window, staying low as you can,

and you have to crawl out onto the fire escape but the ladder
gets stuck and your ma is down there in the alley screaming for help
and you end up hanging from the end of the stuck ladder

and you see Mr. Porter from 3C running and yelling
hang on just hang on in an old T-shirt and pajama pants
till he gets under you and says okay let go now I gotcha

and from three floors up everything down there looks so far away
you don't know if you can make your hands let go but you have to
so finally you do, and he catches you but only sort of,

he falls down, breaks his wrist, and your side gets scraped up so bad
you got scars for life. I'm telling you, if there really *is* a fire,
the only thing you worry about saving is your own sorry skin.

——— ✳ ———

6 5 5 5 9 π

"My laptop. The whole universe on a thirteen-inch screen.
It's like having an extra brain. Besides, they cost a bomb—
just makes sense to pick something expensive over something cheap."

———— * ————

"There's a box on my mom's nightstand.
Inside, wrapped up real careful,
a little curl of brown hair
and some tiny nail clippings.

My brother Anthony's. He'd be eight now, if he were still alive.

His heart, it didn't work right.
I don't remember him much—

I was too little, only four.
But sometimes my mom still cries.

Get hold of that box and run
and keep Anthony safe from the fire."

——— ✳ ———

"It's my job whenever we go out—Mom forgets, she's so busy.
And for sure she'll need her head on straight if there's a fire.
I'd go right to the bathroom and grab her insulin kit."

———— ✳ ————

Shoot. What Sophia said, about her brother who died,
now I can't say what I was gonna say. I'm not stupid,
I know it's way worse to lose a brother than a pet.

But I miss Prince every single day. Him waiting at the window
for me to get home from school, jumping licking happy little barks
like it was years since he's seen me instead of just that morning.

Funny ears, one up, one down. White patches on black fur.
Another dog? Maybe. But it'll never be the same as Prince.
He always *always* thought I was the best. Never doubted on me.

———— ✳ ————

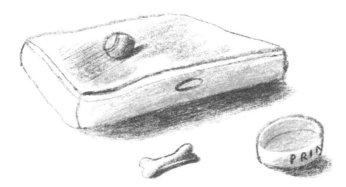

"I've decided: my bookcase.
It's *one* thing, like Nat's collection, right?
Books, game cards, comics,
and the snake skeleton I found last year.
Three hundred and eighteen bones
that I wired together myself."

———— ✳ ————

"Ms. Chang, a whole bookcase? That's not like Natalie's collection—it's all different things. He should have to pick one, if you ask me."

"Yeah, well, who's asking you, Kai?"
"It's just my opinion, Jay, chill!"

"Hmm. I have to agree with Kai that it's stretching things a bit . . . but I'm going to allow it. We're doing this for fun. It's hard, isn't it? I'm having trouble deciding myself."

"Okay, but I still think it's not—um, not in the *spirit* of things."

"Hey, Jay, you could put your bookcase on Charles's rug, ha-ha!"

"Huh. Not if that Richards dude is still rolled up in there."

——— ✳ ———

I keep thinking about Prince, how he never doubted on me.
Well, I'm not doubting on him now. I'll say what I was gonna say:
His collar, from my top drawer. Because it still smells like him.

———— ✳ ————

"What May said about her grans? And that sweater? She made me think.
About *my* gran. There's this photo of her and my abuelo,
who I never knew. Before they were married. She looks so young!

It's a really *old* photo, so that's what I should save, right?
But I gotta be honest, I'm like a hundred percent sure
that if there was a fire, I'd just grab my phone and run."

"Johanna, I have a great idea! Here's what you do:
You take a bunch of pictures of that picture! With your phone!
And then if there's a fire—"
"I'll have both! Cool! Charles, you're a genius!"

———— ✳ ————

"You know, listening to you all, I've changed my mind too.
At first I was going to take my box full of grade books.
Eighteen grade books. Eighteen class pictures. Every student's name—"

"Did you all hear that? She was gonna save us, but now she's not!"
"Not *us*, Sandra. The grade books are just paper, they're not us."
"They're us on paper! She's just gonna leave us to burn up!"

"Excuse me, scholars? I was speaking. Please don't interrupt.
I don't need the grade books to remember you . . . because
you're unforgettable. Don't you ever forget that."

"Ha, Ms. Chang made a joke!"
"Don't forget, we're unforgettable!"

"Okay. Can I finish now?
I think I'd take my philodendron."

"Your filla-what?"
"Philodendron. It's a kind of plant."

"Do you talk to it? 'Cause then maybe it counts as a pet."

"I don't talk to it, but it's special. It grew from a cutting
off my mom's plant. Which grew from a cutting from *her* mom. My gran."

"That's kinda like May's sweater!"

"Yeah, or Johanna's photo."

"Very nice, Ty and Shareen.
Excellent observations,
both astute and profound."

"What does that mean? What's a stoot?"

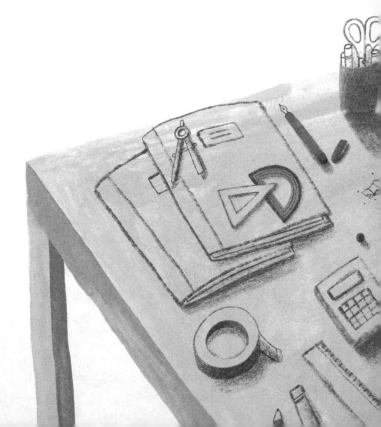

"'Astute,' an adjective. It means sharp, keen, perceptive. 'Profound,' also an adjective. It means wise and deep."

"Are you saying we're deep?"

"Yes. You're the ones who made me change my mind."

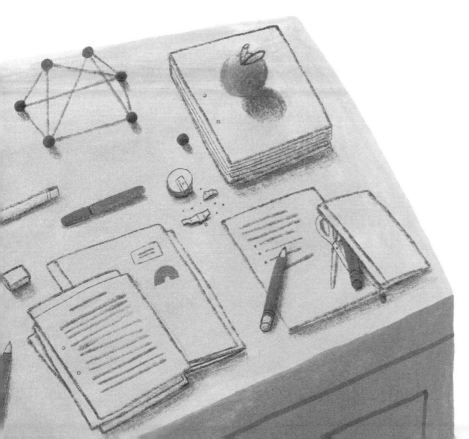

"Ms. Chang, Jay's snake sounds way cool.
Could he maybe bring it to school?"

"What do you think, Jay?"
"Do it, Jay-bird. I'm gonna count all those bones."

"Maybe. I guess I could . . . sure.
You really wanna see it?"

——— ✳ ———

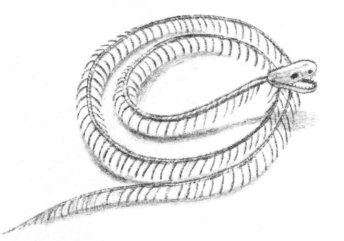

Author's Note

For the poems in this collection, I have borrowed the line structure from sijo. A sijo (pronounced SHEE-zho) is an ancient form of traditional Korean poetry. A classic sijo has three lines of thirteen to seventeen syllables. Sometimes the three lines are divided into six shorter ones. A few of the poems in the book were written using both short and long lines.

All the poems employ the sijo syllabic structure; however, many of them are much longer than traditional sijo. Using old forms in new ways is how poetry continually renews itself, and the world.